Dear Parent:

Congratulations! Your child is taking the first steps on an exciting journey. The destination? Independent reading!

STEP INTO READING® will help your child get there. The program offers five steps to reading success. Each step includes fun stories and colorful art. There are also Step into Reading Sticker Books, Step into Reading Math Readers, Step into Reading Phonics Readers, Step into Reading Write-In Readers, and Step into Reading Phonics Boxed Sets—a complete literacy program with something to interest every child.

Learning to Read, Step by Step!

Ready to Read   Preschool–Kindergarten
• big type and easy words • rhyme and rhythm • picture clues
For children who know the alphabet and are eager to begin reading.

Reading with Help   Preschool–Grade 1
• basic vocabulary • short sentences • simple stories
For children who recognize familiar words and sound out new words with help.

Reading on Your Own   Grades 1–3
• engaging characters • easy-to-follow plots • popular topics
For children who are ready to read on their own.

Reading Paragraphs   Grades 2–3
• challenging vocabulary • short paragraphs • exciting stories
For newly independent readers who read simple sentences with confidence.

Ready for Chapters   Grades 2–4
• chapters • longer paragraphs • full-color art
For children who want to take the plunge into chapter books but still like colorful pictures.

STEP INTO READING® is designed to give every child a successful reading experience. The grade levels are only guides. Children can progress through the steps at their own speed, developing confidence in their reading, no matter what their grade.

Remember, a lifetime love of reading starts with a single step!

For Allie and Benjamin—M.M.-K.

Visit us on the Web!
StepIntoReading.com
randomhouse.com/kids
www.barbie.com

Educators and librarians, for a variety of teaching tools, visit us at randomhouse.com/teachers

ISBN 978-0-375-97030-6 (trade) — ISBN 978-0-307-93033-0 (lib. bdg.)
Printed in the United States of America   10 9 8 7

Barbie i can be...
A Horse Rider

Concept developed for Mattel by Egmont Creative Center

Adapted by Mary Man-Kong

Illustrated by JiYoung An and TJ Team

Random House 🏠 New York

Barbie and her sister
Chelsea love horses.

Barbie can ride a horse
in many ways!

Barbie twirls a rope.

She ropes a cow.

Barbie rides
around a barrel.

Barbie loves
her horse, Tawny.

Barbie takes Chelsea
to the stable.

Barbie teaches Chelsea.

They saddle Starlight.

Chelsea's class goes on a trail ride.

Barbie teaches Tawny.
They trot!

They jump!

Tawny will not jump
over the log fence.

Barbie tells Tawny it will be okay.

Tawny will still
not jump.

Barbie and her friends
get small logs.

Barbie makes
a small log fence.

Barbie keeps
Tawny calm.

Tawny jumps
over the log fence!

Where is Chelsea?

Barbie must find
her sister!

Barbie finds a clue.
It is Chelsea's ribbon.

A big log is
in Barbie's way.

Tawny jumps
over the log!

Barbie finds Chelsea!

She is safe.

Chelsea is proud
of Barbie.

Barbie is proud
of Tawny.

Barbie is a good
horse rider!